# WELCOME TO DINOSAUR SCHOOL

Written by
**Rose Cobden**

Illustrated by
**Loretta Schauer**

All through the land, little dinos were stirring.

They opened their eyes, and their brains started whirring.

**"The BIG day is here!"** they thought from their beds . . . .
Some leapt with excitement, some trembled with dread.

One little dino woke up with a start.

As she lay in her bed, she felt scared in her heart.

"It's time to get up,"
Papa called out to Jewel.

"You don't want to miss your
**first day at school!**"

Jewel trudged down the stairs with an anxious *galumph* . . .

She chomped through her breakfast, then picked up her lunch.

She brushed her sharp teeth and polished her scales,

then reached for her jumper that hung on the rail.

Jewel stepped out the door,
holding tight to Dad's hand.
Her shiny new shoes slipped
about in the sand.

First-day dinos rushed by,
racing fast towards school.

Some **plodded,**

some **skipped** . . .

some looked really **cool!**

They reached the school gates, which flew open wide,
and a teacher appeared. "I am your school guide.
Let's be mega-Stegas – not Ptera-fools!
Come on in, and . . .

welcome to
Dinosaur
School!"

Jewel waved bye to Papa; Dad kissed her forehead.

She walked in with a smile (that she hoped hid her dread).

The classroom was **BIG** – it smelled clean and new.
Jewel patiently waited to be told what to do!

The dinos were each given pegs for their bags.
They knew whose was whose by the small picture tags.

The teacher then listed their
names one by one,
and when Jewel was called,
she wanted to run.

The teacher then said,
    "You're nervous, I'm sure.
But follow me, there's lots to see –
    it's time for your **school tour!**

We have lava pits for playtime . . .

and stones to carve for art . . .

dino-loos for little poos . . .

and lots of work to start!"

Next the scaly classmates were sorted into tables and given drawers for their work, marked with dino-labels.

Jewel sat next to Roary,
who towered like a tree.
"School is **great!** Don't you think?"
But Jewel did not agree.

Jewel's tummy rumbled loudly when the bell rang out for lunch.
The dining hall was noisy.

Slurp!

Chomp!

Crunch

She wasn't sure where to sit,
or even what to do.

But Roary shouted,

**"Here, Jewel.**

**I've saved a seat for you!"**

Then the class went out to the rough and rocky yard –
little dinos **running wild**, racing fast and hard!

Roary called to his new friend,

**"Come on, Jewel.
Let's play!"**

As she ran, Jewel forgot
the nerves of her first day.

After play, it was back to class and time to make some art.
Paints and rocks were handed round so the class could start.

An excited Jewel began to splash colours here and there.
*School is really fun!* she thought as **paint flew everywhere!**

Now to tidy up and clear away the muck and grime.

Then the class sat on the mat for dino-story time.

The two new friends high-fived as their first day at school was done.
The teacher handed out their bags.

**"Goodbye, everyone!"**

Dad was waiting outside when Jewel ran out the gate.

She spotted him and shouted,

**"My first school day was GREAT!"**

"Your second will be better," Dad said,
handing her a snack.
Jewel looked at him, confused.

"You mean . . .
I have to
go back?"

# Look out for more
# Ladybird picture books . . .

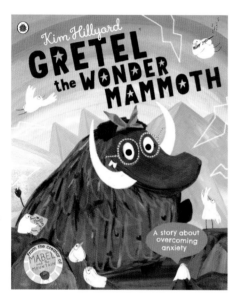

☐ 9780241488560

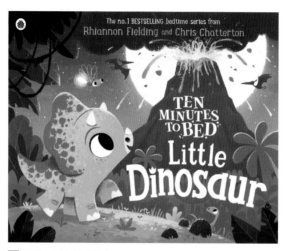

☐ 9780241386736

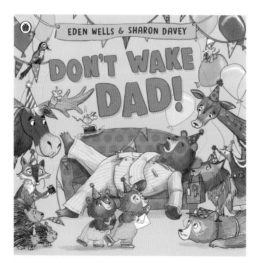

☐ 9780241560594

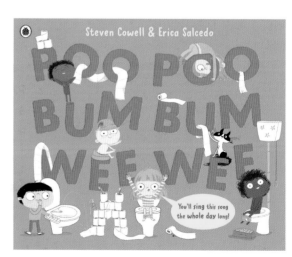

☐ 9780241473085